For Tommy, Billy, Emma and Katie – J.D.

First published in 2000 by Macmillan Children's Books
A division of Macmillan Publishers Limited
20 New Wharf Road, London N1 9RR
Basingstoke and Oxford
Associated companies throughout the world
This edition produced 2004 for The Book People Ltd,
Hall Wood Avenue, Haydock, St Helens WA11 9UL

ISBN 0 333 72000 8

Text copyright © 2000 Julia Donaldson
Illustrations © 2000 Axel Scheffler

5 7 9 8 6 4

A CIP catalogue record for this book is available from the British Library.

Printed in China

Julia Donaldson   Axel Scheffler

Monkey
Puzzle

TED SMART

"I've lost my mum!"

"Hush, little monkey, don't you cry.
I'll help you find her," said Butterfly.
"Let's have a think. How big is she?"

"She's big!" said the monkey. "Bigger than me."

"Bigger than you? Then I've seen your mum.
Come, little monkey, come, come, come."

"No, no, no! That's an elephant.

"My mum isn't a great grey hunk.
She hasn't got tusks or a curly trunk.
She doesn't have great thick baggy knees.
And anyway, *her* tail coils round trees."

"She coils round trees? Then she's very near.
Quick, little monkey! She's over here."

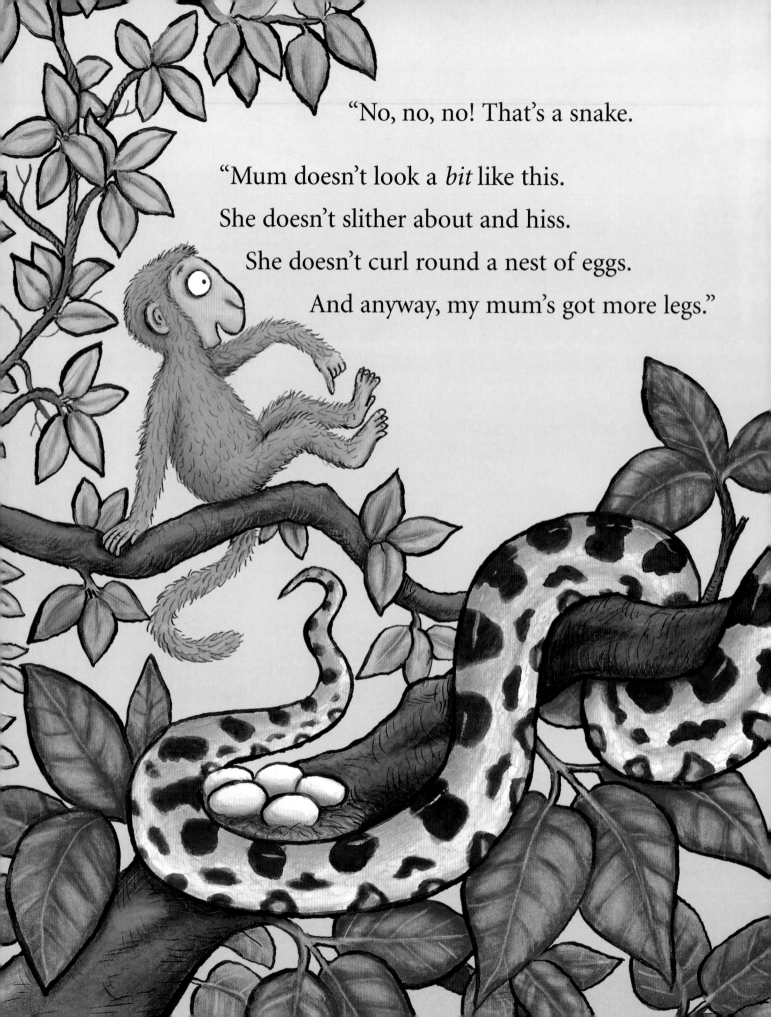

"No, no, no! That's a snake.

"Mum doesn't look a *bit* like this.

She doesn't slither about and hiss.

She doesn't curl round a nest of eggs.

And anyway, my mum's got more legs."

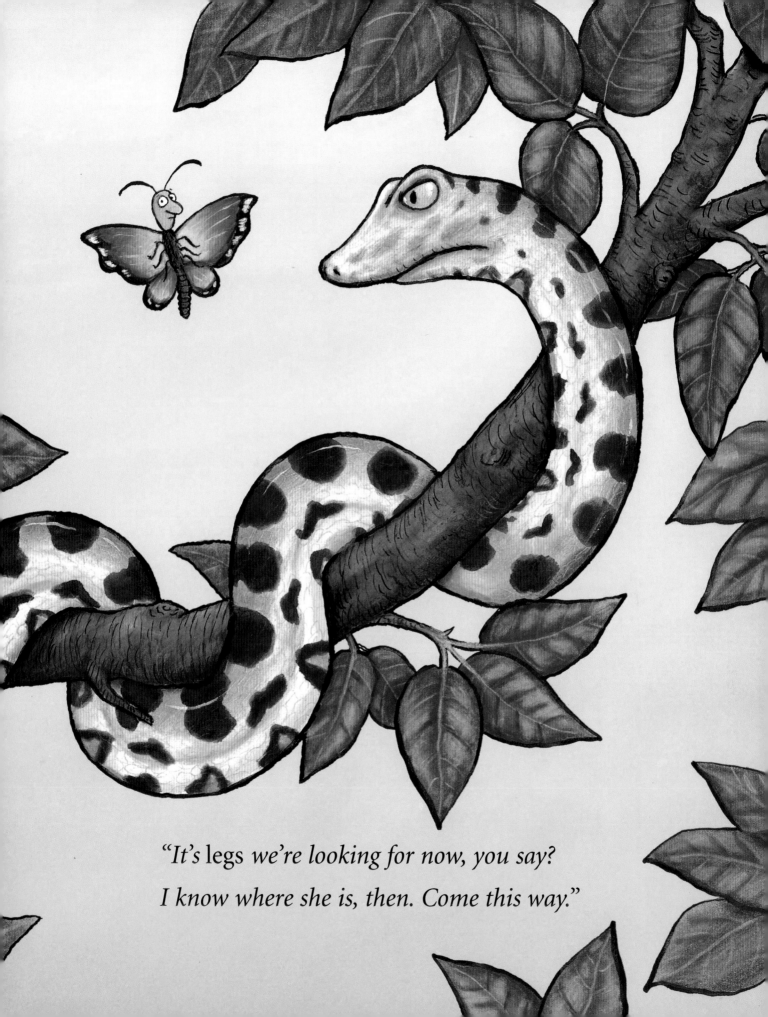

"It's legs we're looking for now, you say?
I know where she is, then. Come this way."

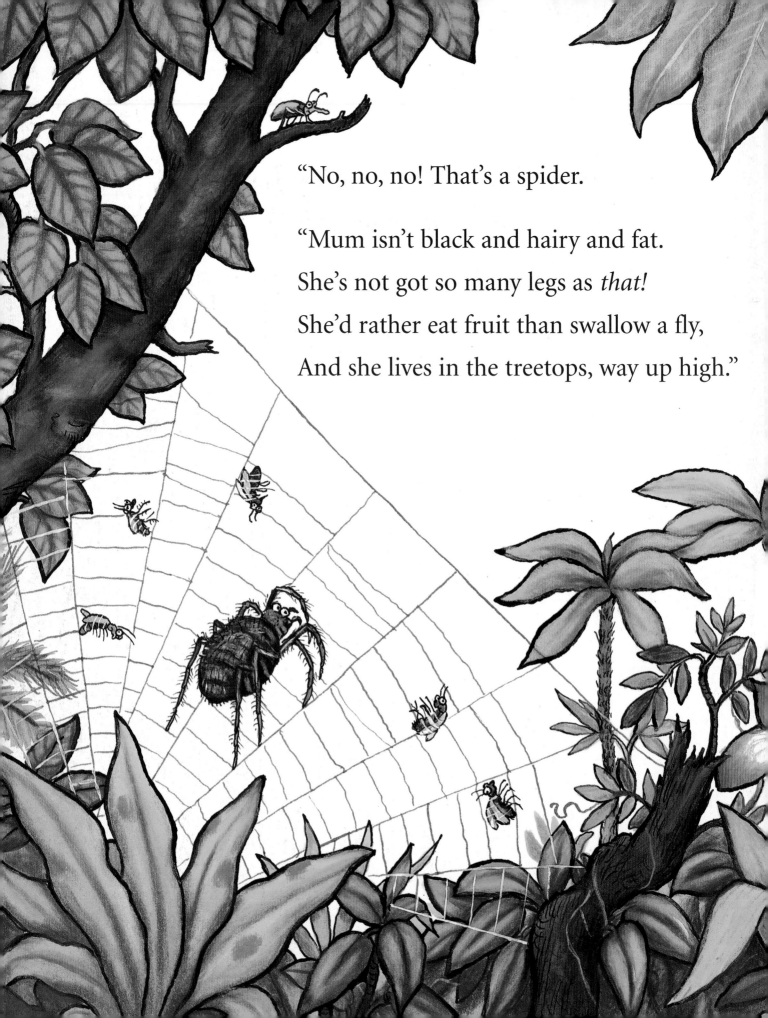

"No, no, no! That's a spider.

"Mum isn't black and hairy and fat.
She's not got so many legs as *that!*
She'd rather eat fruit than swallow a fly,
And she lives in the treetops, way up high."

"She lives in the trees? You should have said!
Your mummy's hiding above your head."

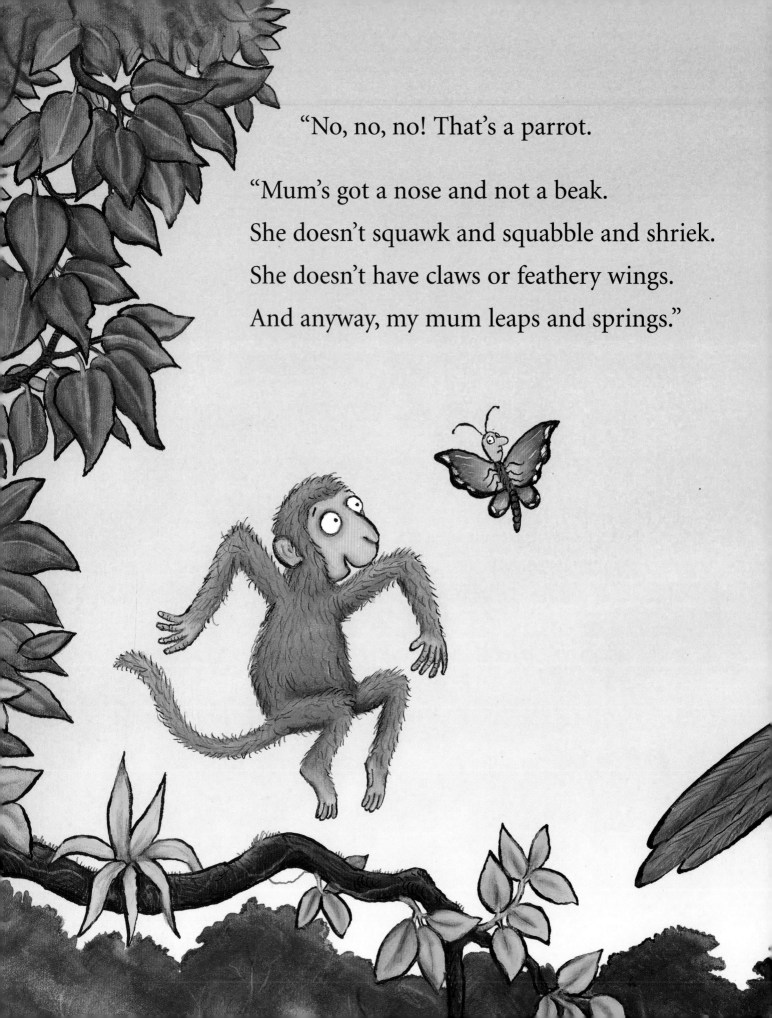

"No, no, no! That's a parrot.

"Mum's got a nose and not a beak.

She doesn't squawk and squabble and shriek.

She doesn't have claws or feathery wings.

And anyway, my mum leaps and springs."

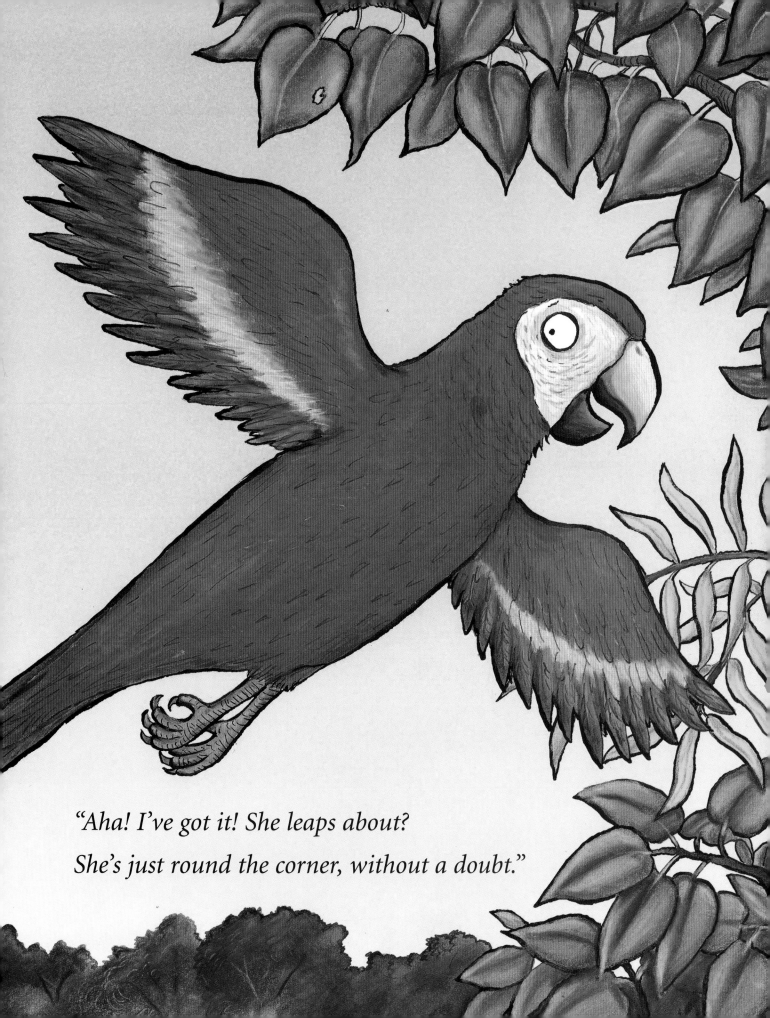

"Aha! I've got it! She leaps about?
She's just round the corner, without a doubt."

"No, no, no! That's a frog!

"Butterfly, butterfly, please don't joke!
Mum's not green and she doesn't croak.
She's not all slimy. Oh dear, what a muddle!
She's brown and furry, and nice to cuddle."

"Brown fur – why didn't you tell me so?
We'll find her in no time – off we go!"

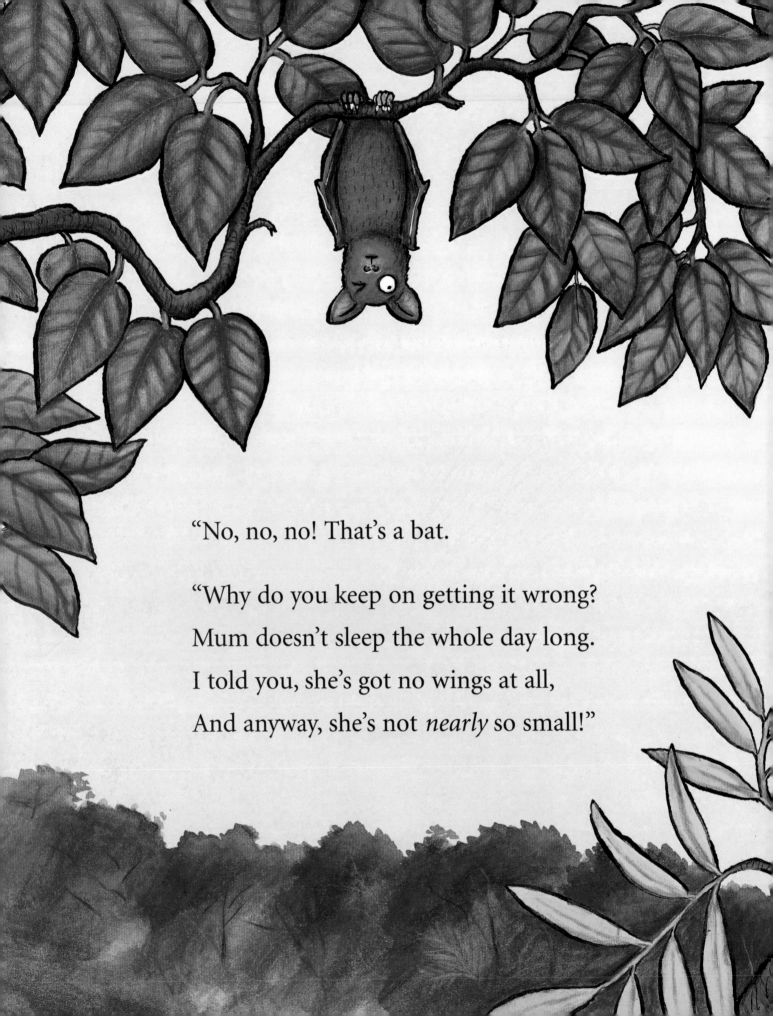

"No, no, no! That's a bat.

"Why do you keep on getting it wrong?
Mum doesn't sleep the whole day long.
I told you, she's got no wings at all,
And anyway, she's not *nearly* so small!"

"Your mum's not little? Now let me think.
She's down by the river, having a drink!"

"NO, NO, NO!
That's the elephant again!

"Butterfly, butterfly, can't you see?
None of these creatures looks like me!"

"*You never told me she looked like you!*"

"Of course I didn't! I thought you knew!"

"*I didn't know. I couldn't! You see . . .*

"... None of my babies looks like me.
So she looks like you! Well, if that's the case
We'll soon discover her hiding place."

"No, no, no! That's my dad!

"Come, little monkey, come, come, come.
It's time I took you home to . . ."

"Mum!"